For Grant, Mark and Tammy
J.F.

For Jem, Anne, Benjamin and Rose
P.M.

Text copyright © 1992 by Jenni Fleetwood
Illustrations copyright © 1992 by Peter Melnyczuk
First published in Great Britain by J.M. Dent & Sons Ltd.

First U.S. Edition   1   2   3   4   5   6   7   8   9   10

Library of Congress Cataloging in Publication Data
Fleetwood, Jenni. While shepherds watched / by Jenni Fleetwood; illustrations by Peter Melnyczuk.
p.   cm.   Summary: Present at the birth of a baby lamb, eight-year-old Matthias also witnesses another birth in the city of Bethlehem.   ISBN 0-688-11598-5. —ISBN 0-688-11599-3 (lib. bdg.)
1. Jesus Christ—Juvenile fiction.   [1. Jesus Christ—Nativity—Fiction.]   I. Melnyczuk, Peter, ill.
II. Title.   PZ7.F59864Wh   1992   [E]—dc20   91-38779   CIP   AC

WHILE SHEPHERDS WATCHED

by Jenni Fleetwood
illustrated by Peter Melnyczuk

Lothrop, Lee & Shepard Books
New York

Matthias shivered with excitement. Today was his birthday. He was eight years old, and tonight, for the first time, he would spend all night in the fields with the other shepherds.

It got dark suddenly. One minute Matthias could clearly see the rocks and tussocks of grass on the hillside; the next, even the sheep were just shadows. He pulled his sheepskin jerkin closer and felt for the satisfying shape of his new whistle. His father had carved it as a present, and Matthias was very proud of it.

The sheep were drawing closer together, huddling for warmth in the lee of the wall. But one sheep stood apart from the rest.

"What's the matter with that one?" Matthias asked.

John, who was four years older than Matthias, laughed. "Never seen a lamb born, Matt?" he asked.

Matthias shook his head.

The older boy's face softened. "You'll see it tonight," he said. "That ewe is ready to give birth. That's why she has moved away from the group."

Matthias's heart skipped a beat. A lamb born on his birthday! It was the best present of all.

It was almost midnight when the lamb was born. Matthias watched the exhausted ewe lick her baby gently, but even when it was clean, the lamb made no sound and did not try to get to its feet.

Was something wrong with it? Matthias worried. He wished there were more light so he could better see the lamb.

Then suddenly there *was* light, a light so radiant that it threw the whole field into sharp focus. Below them, Bethlehem looked as it always did—a hamlet of honey-gold houses. But the light did not come from Bethlehem; it seemed to be pouring from the sky itself. And from the light, there stepped a white and clear and brilliant figure, like nothing Matthias had ever seen before.

The shepherds were frightened, but Matthias was too concerned about the lamb to feel afraid.

The figure spoke: "Fear not," it said, "for behold, I bring you good tidings of great joy. Unto you is born this day in the city of David a Savior, which is Christ the Lord. Ye shall find the babe wrapped in swaddling clothes, lying in a manger."

The sound of singing was all around them as the figure faded, but the light did not go. The field remained bright, and when he looked up, Matthias saw a star shining over Bethlehem, the place that people called the city of David.

At first the shepherds were silent. Then everyone was speaking at once.

"What was that?"

"Was it an angel?"

"Is it true about this special baby?"

Then John's voice, louder than the rest, called: "Let us go and see!"

"Yes," the others agreed. "Let us follow the star to Bethlehem!"

Matthias, too, felt a strange yearning to follow the star. But the lamb was shivering, its head on his knee. He could not leave it behind.

As the shepherds hurried toward Bethlehem, Matthias sat playing his whistle and thinking. Suddenly he made up his mind. Opening his jerkin, he tucked the little lamb against his chest. Then he closed his coat and drew the string tight to keep the little creature safe.

The starlight made it easy to follow the path. When he caught up with the others, they were already entering the town.

"They say the baby lies in a stable," John told him.

"But a stable is for animals," said Matthias, hugging the lamb closer.

"There was no room in the inn," John explained.

They joined a stream of
townsfolk pressing down the
dusty track. When they reached
the stable, they were part of quite
a crowd. Matthias hung back, but
the people behind were pushing
hard, and he was soon jostled
through the doorway.

It was just an ordinary stable,
but the starlight was so bright that
Matthias could see every detail.
Ever afterward he could picture it
clearly in his memory.

There were a donkey and a cow and a few goats. Hay stood in bales, its sweet scent filling the air. In a corner, bathed in the yellow glow of candlelight, sat a family—a father, and a mother holding a tiny baby.

Matthias wanted to see the child, but there were too many people in front of him and he was not very tall. Forgetting for a moment the lamb against his chest, he jumped.

The baby's mother looked up. Seeing Matthias, she asked the others to move so that he might come closer.

The baby looked like any baby. It was wrapped in plain cloth. What a disappointment! Matthias didn't know what he had expected, but certainly not this.

He leaned forward, and as he did, his jerkin fell open. The lamb—so small, so weak, still wet from birth—peeked out.

"It's just been born," Matthias told the woman.

"Like my son," she answered softly.

Then the baby reached out and touched the lamb. Matthias felt something fizz inside him—such a happy feeling, it took him by surprise.

Suddenly he wanted to give the child something, but what? And then he remembered his birthday whistle. He put it in the manger.

"Thank you." The baby's mother smiled.

Matthias's heart felt so full, he thought he must burst. Jumping up, he raced out of the stable. Up the path he ran, to the fields, the lamb bumping softly against him.

A dark shape stood by the gate—it was the ewe. Gently, Matthias opened his jerkin and set the lamb on the ground. It looked around for a moment, took a couple of shaky steps, then moved quickly to its mother, its small tail wagging.

Matthias watched as the ewe nudged her healthy little lamb toward her milk. Then he looked back over his shoulder. The town of Bethlehem, the city of David, lay still and silent beneath the silver light of the star.

"It's been a night for miracles," Matthias whispered.